Davy Crockett and the Wild Cat

written by
Sharon Fear

illustrated by
Chuck Muchow

HARCOURT BRACE & COMPANY

Orlando   Atlanta   Austin   Boston   San Francisco   Chicago   Dallas   New York
Toronto   London

Well, that did it! That cat was in LOVE! That cat was as sweet as a kitten.

And he could make a Wild Cat into a Kitty Cat.